Together in Death

Contents

1

The Move

It was Dad's idea to move.
He'd wanted to get away ever since Mum died.
Our house had too many memories.

'I've got a new job,' he said one day.
'I'll be working for Charles Treffor
who owns a big estate.
I'll be planting saplings and
cutting down dead trees. That kind of thing.'

Dad worked for the parks department
in our town. He liked being out of doors.
In winter, if he couldn't go out,
he was like a bear with a sore head.
'There's a cottage with the job,' he said.
'And you'll be able to get to college, Luke.
There's a bus route not far away.'

In September, I was starting my final year
in Forestry Studies. I was just like Dad.
I liked plants and being out in the open air.
'I don't see why we have to move,' said Beth.
'I want to stay here.'
(My sister can be a pain sometimes.)
Dad put his arm around her.
'You'll like the house, Beth,' he said.
'It's on the edge of a wood.'
She gazed up at him with her big brown eyes.
I knew what was coming.
'Will you let me borrow the car, then?'
she said. 'I'll need to go and see my friends.'
Dad sighed and agreed.
He always gave in to Beth.

We moved in July.
I liked the cottage as soon as I saw it.
It had a big kitchen
and a square living room downstairs.
Upstairs, there were three bedrooms
tucked under the eaves.
From mine, I could see the wood.
Brilliant! I thought.
Every morning I'd wake up
to the sound of birdsong.
Every night I'd fall asleep
to the sound of owls hooting.

But as I lay in bed that first night,
it wasn't owls I heard.
It was something much more sinister.
It was a long, painful howling
from deep in the wood.
It made the blood in my veins run cold.

2

The Howling

'Didn't you sleep well, Luke?'
asked Dad the next morning.
I reached for some toast. 'Terrible,' I said.
'That howling. It never stopped.'
'What howling?' said Beth,
looking up from her cereal.
'Didn't you hear it?'
'No. I didn't hear a thing,' she said.
'You must have been dreaming!'

Dad turned and looked at me.
'What kind of howling was it?'
It was hard to describe.
'It was like an animal in pain,' I said,
'or angry … I don't know.'
Beth raised her eyebrows
and returned to her breakfast.
'It sounds like a fox,' Dad said.
'There must be plenty around here.
Better get used to them.'

We spent most of the day unpacking.
By the middle of the afternoon
we were all fed up with putting things away.
We wanted to do something different.
'You two go off for a walk or something,'
Dad said.
'I'll have a cup of tea and put my feet up.'
We decided to go into the wood.
It seemed like a good idea.
But that was when it all began.
That was the first time we saw them.

3

Keeper's Lodge

'Race you!' said Beth and we ran down
the back garden and into the wood.
We followed a narrow path that led us
through a copse of oak saplings and birches.
Sometimes, brambles blocked our way
and scratched at our legs.
As we got deep into the wood,
the trees grew close together.
There was a chill in the air now.
We walked on, not saying much –
just following the path.

We went round a bend, and Beth stopped.
'What's that building over there?' she said.
I looked across and saw something
dimly in the distance.
'Probably a keeper's lodge.
The estate's very old.
A gamekeeper would have lived there years ago.
He'd watch for poachers
and look after the birds.'
Beth wanted to go and look.
We walked towards the cottage.

It was then that we heard dogs barking.
These were no pets. They sounded fierce.
Suddenly two dogs appeared
from the back of the cottage.
Large and black and vicious.
Growling and baring their teeth.
We froze on the spot. I hardly dared speak.
'Run for it, Beth!' I whispered.

She didn't need telling.
She was already racing back towards the path.
I tore after her ... and so did the dogs.
I could hear them getting closer all the time.
I ran on until my lungs screamed to stop.
Then suddenly, near the edge of the wood,
the dogs stopped. We could hardly believe it.
They whined, turned and
trotted back towards the cottage.
I flopped against a tree, gasping air,
grateful to feel the warm sun again.
Beth was slumped on the ground,
her head resting on her knees.

'Phew!' I said. 'They were a bit nasty.'
Slowly, she looked up. 'I suppose those dogs
could have been howling in the night,'
she said.
'Maybe. Let's hope it doesn't happen
too often.'

We walked around the edge of the wood
and found a road leading down to a village.
'Let's have a drink in that pub,'
Beth suggested. 'My throat's parched.'

The locals were friendly enough.
We got talking about Dad.
'So he'll be working in the wood then?'
the landlord said as he wiped the counter.
'You tell him to watch out.'
'What do you mean – watch out?' I said.
One of the drinkers leaned forwards.
'Some funny goings on,' he said,
tapping the side of his nose.
'You want to be careful.'

'There was a murder, you know,' said another.
'Over by Keeper's Lodge.'
'Is that the cottage in the wood?'
'Aye,' he said.
'But nobody goes near the wood.'
Beth wasn't impressed. 'That's not true!
Somebody lives there!' she said. 'We saw …'
The oldest of them wagged his finger.
'No,' he said. 'Nobody's lived there
since the murder. I tell'ee. Keep away.'

4

A Visit

A few days later, Dad went to the county show
with Charles Treffor.
'Mr Treffor wants us to stay over
in Worcester for two nights,' said Dad.
'We'll be coming back on Friday.
Will you two be OK by yourselves?'
That's Dad for you!
He still thinks we need looking after.
'We'll be fine, Dad!' Beth said.
'Don't worry. Just go and have a good time.'

That night we generally lazed around.
We watched TV. Ate a curry out of the freezer.
By ten o'clock, I'd started to yawn.
'I'm going to bed,' I said. 'I'm shattered.'
Beth was watching a film.
'OK,' she said, without looking up.
'See you in the morning.'

I really needed a good night's sleep.
Ever since we'd moved in, I'd slept badly.
It was the howling!
You'd think I'd get used to it.
But no! I heard it every night.
And it seemed to get louder.
By the time I'd got undressed,
I could hardly keep my eyes open.
I slipped under the duvet
and let my head drop onto the pillow.
Fantastic! I was warm and very comfortable.
I began to drift into a deep sleep.
But some time later, I was awoken by a noise.
It wasn't the howling this time.
It was different. I listened carefully.

At first, there was just the rustle of trees.
Then, there was something nearer.
Something at the foot of my bed!
It was breathing. No! Something more. Panting!

I sat up in bed and switched on the light.
There – between my bed and the window –
were the two dogs. They were staring at me
with powerful green eyes. They panted.
Their tongues lolled out of their mouths.
Any minute they were going to leap.

I screamed. I jumped out of bed
and grabbed for the doorknob.
In a flash, I was on the landing,
slamming the door behind me.
'Beth!' I yelled. 'Beth!' I scrambled down
the stairs into the living room.
'What on earth's wrong with you?' she said.
She was really annoyed. She hated being
interrupted when she was watching a film.
My face must have been as white as a sheet.
'Luke, what's happened?' she said.

I leaned against the door.
'You're not going to believe this,' I said.
'Try me.'
I sighed. 'OK. But I warn you …
I'm not sure I believe it.'
'What?'
'Those two dogs we saw in the wood …'
'Yes?'
'… they're in my bedroom.'

Beth's mouth fell open. 'They can't be!
You're just having a nightmare.'
'I wasn't asleep,' I said.
There was no way I could prove it –
unless we went to look.

We crept upstairs and stood outside my room.
'Don't open the door, Beth,' I said. 'Listen.'
There was no doubt about it.
We could hear panting.
From time to time there was a whine.
The dogs were in there sure enough.
'So,' said Beth. 'What do we do now?'

5

Thomas Wilson

We decided to wait until morning.
Then we'd telephone the police.
They'd come and sort it out.
That night, I slept on the floor
in Beth's room.
Somehow, neither of us wanted to be alone.
In the end, we didn't need to call the police.
As soon as it was light, we got up
and listened outside my bedroom door.
No noise. Not a sound. We turned the handle
and pushed the door open – ever so slightly.

We peeped through the gap.
No dogs as far as we could see.
So we opened the door wider and looked in.
The dogs had gone. Definitely!
'Maybe we were both mistaken,' said Beth.
'Come on. Let's go down and have breakfast.'

We lazed around for a bit, drinking coffee.
We weren't even dressed
when somebody knocked at the door.
'Good morning!' the man said.
'I didn't get you out of bed did I?'
He turned out to be the Vicar!

'Come in,' I said. 'I'll make some coffee.'
He'd come to see Dad really.
I explained he was away.
'I just wanted to welcome you to the parish,'
he said. 'I hope you'll be very happy here.'
He was really friendly and we got on well.
In fact, we got on so well he conned us
into mowing the grass around the church
that afternoon.

'The man who usually does it,' he explained,
'has a problem with his back.
I'm sure he'll be fine by next week.'
I found out later how he'd hurt his back!
That mower must have been fifty years old.

At three o' clock, the Vicar came over
with some orange juice and cake.
Somehow, we got talking about our visit to
the pub. Then we asked him about the murder.
'That was before my time, of course,' he said.
'It was never proved.
They never found the body.'
'So who was murdered?'
'They say it was the gamekeeper,
Thomas Wilson.
He lived in the wood with his wife.
They say poachers shot him. But I can't say.
His wife died of a broken heart.
She's buried just here. See!'
He pointed to a small headstone nearby.

We bent over to read the words.
JANE WILSON
1895–1920
BELOVED WIFE OF THOMAS

'She was only young then,' Beth said.
'That's terrible.'
'No children,' I said.
'No,' said the Vicar.
'But the dogs are buried under that tree.'
'Dogs?'
'Yes they had two. Come and look.'

By the edge of the graveyard
was a small square stone.
BLACKIE AND THUNDER
FAITHFUL UNTO DEATH

I felt shaky. Beth glanced over at me.
We were both thinking the same thing.
The dogs in the wood.
They were Blackie and Thunder.
'Why "Faithful unto death?"' I asked.

'The dogs were shot and left in the wood.
They probably died trying to protect
Thomas Wilson from the poachers.
The villagers wanted the dogs buried here.
They were very special.'
We couldn't wait to be by ourselves.
'The dogs are ghosts,' said Beth.
'And I don't think they're vicious at all.'
'Then why did they follow us?' I said.
That was the question.
What was it the dogs wanted?

6

Blackie and Thunder

We thought the dogs
would come back that night.
Ghosts come out at night. They need the dark.
'It makes sense,' said Beth.
'We saw them in the wood where it was dark.
When we got to the edge – in the sunlight –
they turned back. Remember?'
'Right!' I said. 'We'll go to my room later.
We'll wait and see if they turn up.'
We were both nervous.
Neither of us could eat any tea.

We watched TV for a bit
but we both kept looking at our watches.
We kept looking at the window.
Waiting for the light to fade.
By nine o'clock it was dusk.
We went upstairs and sat on my bed –
facing the window.
'They must come that way,' I said.
'That's where I saw them last night.'
Beth didn't answer.
'Just supposing we're wrong.
Supposing the dogs are vicious after all.
What if they tear us to pieces?'

We finally agreed we'd be crazy
to wait there like sitting ducks.
We had to have some kind of protection.
Dad had a gun. It was locked away
but I knew where the key was.
'I'll go and get it,' I said.
'If things get bad, I'll shoot.'
I left her alone in the bedroom.
'I'll only be a minute,' I said.

I hurried across the landing into Dad's room.
Some keys were in the top drawer of the chest.
I tried three of the most likely looking ones.
The first one didn't fit.
Then the second one got jammed in the lock.
I struggled until the key finally came loose.
Then I put in the third.
I unlocked the cupboard
and lifted the gun out.
But where was the ammunition?
I opened drawers. I looked under the bed.
Then I found it on top of the wardrobe.
Quickly, I loaded the gun
and set the safety catch.
'I've got it, Beth!' I called.
'We'll be OK now, whatever happens.'
But there was no reply.

I was filled with panic
as I raced across the landing.
I flung back the door and raised the gun.
Beth was sitting on the bed as I'd left her.
She was white faced and staring straight ahead.

I turned and knew what I would see.

Just as before, the dogs were standing there.

I raised the gun.

'D–don't!' Beth stuttered.

She could hardly move her lips for fear.

I wanted to blow them away. Get rid of them.

Instead, I edged my way slowly next to Beth.

'Th–they came when you'd left,' she whispered, her eyes fixed on the dogs.

'I don't think they mean any harm.

Don't shoot.'

I stared at them.

For a while, they stared back.

Then they began to move towards the bed.

My fingers gripped the trigger of the gun.

They came close. I could hear their panting.

'I've got to do something,' I hissed.

'Wait,' said Beth. 'Please.'

As she spoke the bigger of the two dogs suddenly grabbed at my arm.

'No!' I yelled and tried to pull away.

But I soon realised it wasn't biting me.

It had grabbed hold of my sleeve
and was pulling me off the bed.
The other dog was doing the same to Beth.
They led us downstairs and out of the cottage.
'They're taking us somewhere,' she said.
'I don't think they mean us any harm.'

Beth was right.
They were leading us into the wood …
to Keeper's Lodge … and beyond.
Then, in a small clearing, they stopped.
'What are they doing?' Beth whispered.
The dogs began to dig.
They scratched frantically.
They dug a hole half a metre deep.
We could see very little in the darkness.
When the dogs stepped back from the hole,
we spotted something in the earth.
Something round and white.
'What is it?' said Beth.
I bent down and reached into the hole.
As my fingers curled around it,
I knew for sure it was Thomas Wilson's skull.

8

Together in Death

The next morning, we dialled 999.
When Dad got back from Worcester, the wood
was swarming with police and reporters.
They dug up the bones and proved
the remains belonged to Thomas Wilson.
He'd been shot in the head.
Probably by poachers.
We were heroes in the village.
We had found the missing body.
Everyone wanted to hear our story.

The police didn't believe the part
about the ghost dogs. But the locals did.
They'd all seen the dogs in the wood,
but they'd always run from them –
just as we had that first day.
'They looked so fierce,'
said the landlord of the pub.
'We thought they were killers.'

When the police had finished,
the villagers asked the vicar
to hold a burial service.
They wanted to bury Thomas with his wife.
Some weeks later, we watched as the remains
of Thomas Wilson were lowered into the ground.
TOGETHER IN DEATH read the new
headstone.

That evening, Beth and I
went back to the grave.
Beth placed some flowers
on the newly dug earth.
As we stood, we saw a movement
at the edge of the graveyard.

We turned and saw Blackie and Thunder
pounding across the grass.
We bent down to greet them,
but they ran straight past us.
What we saw next was unbelievable.
The dogs were leaping up
at a man and a woman, standing not far away.
They were not of our world.
Somehow, we weren't afraid.
We just watched as Thomas and Jane
walked away, hand in hand.
The dogs running behind.
Together in death.